Margret & H. A. Rey's

Curiously Calm

with

Curious George®

Written by Dawn Huebner, PhD

This is George.

He is a good little monkey
and always very **curious**.

George feels **curious** every day.

He also feels
happy,
sad,
excited,
angry,
scared,
and
calm.

George is glad to have so many feelings,
especially the ones that feel **good**.

But not all of George's feelings feel good.

In fact, some of his feelings are
quite unpleasant.

George knows he can't
make these feelings go away.

But he can make them smaller.

The best way to make an
unpleasant feeling smaller is to

breathe.

But George already
breathes all the time!

He breathes when he is **angry**,
and when he is **frightened**,
and when he is **sad**.

He breathes when he is awake and asleep.
And still, he sometimes feels **bad**.

The kind of
breathing George does
all day and all night won't
help him with his feelings.

But **SPECIAL**
breathing will.

George thinks about something he loves—
CAKE.
The cake is covered
in frosting and candles.

He breathes in slowly
and deeply through his nose.
His imaginary cake smells wonderful!

Then **whooooooosh**—
George lets out
all his breath.

Blowing out imaginary
candles makes George feel better,
so he decides to do it again.

Sniff...

...***whooooooosh***!

He wonders what else he can do
to make unpleasant feelings smaller.

He can try different things for
different feelings.

When George feels **angry**,
he can **walk away**.

He can also **play with a pet**.
Their soft fur helps him feel peaceful.

And he can **talk to a trusted friend**,
especially one who listens well.

But what about when he is **scared**?

When George is scared, he can try to be **BRAVE**.

But sometimes that is hard.

When George is alone or doing something he's never done before,

he doesn't
feel brave at all.

When he is **scared**,

there is another trick George can try.

He can do just a bit of the hard thing.

And then just a little bit more.

George feels **PROUD** of himself when he is brave.

George is curious about one more feeling.
It's the way he feels when he makes a mistake,

or
his friends
are too busy
to play,

or things don't go
the way he wanted.

When George feels **sad**,
he can take some **special breaths**.

He can **talk to
someone he loves**.

And then he can **do something fun**.
George can:

Make something.

Play a game.

Look at his favorite book.

But George doesn't feel sad right now.
He doesn't feel angry, and
he doesn't feel scared.

After thinking about so many feelings,
George feels tired!

But he knows just what to do about that.

He can rest and
eat a healthy snack

and find pictures
in the clouds.

So that's what George does.

And then he
FEELS BETTER.

Learning to be Curiously Calm
by Dawn Huebner, PhD

All feelings are normal, even those that are unpleasant. The goal is never to hurry children out of feeling sad, or angry, or jealous, or frustrated—which simply doesn't work—but instead to equip them with strategies for coping. Reading books like *Curiously Calm with Curious George* can help. Here are six more things you can do with your child to help them learn to regulate their emotions:

1. Manage your own emotions. Children learn self-regulation by seeing it in action in the adults around them. Model the strategies you are trying to teach.

2. Talk about feelings—yours, theirs, and everyone's. Watch for opportunities to name and normalize both positive and negative feelings.

3. Help your child recognize what they are feeling by narrating what you see. For example, "Your hands are clenched, and you're using a loud voice. You seem angry."

4. Validate and accept all feelings. You may not agree with the feeling, but it makes sense from your child's perspective. Let your child know that you see them and you understand their emotional experience.

5. Empathize with what your child is feeling. "You keep trying and trying, and it still isn't working. That's frustrating!" Empathy is calming to the brain, renewing access to logical thinking and problem-solving.

6. Teach specific coping skills. Expect to say, "Let's take some breaths together," many, many times before this skill is internalized. The same goes for taking a break, cuddling a stuffed animal, doing a quiet activity, or eating a healthy snack. Move from using the coping skill with your child, to reminding them, to having them access the skill on their own.